I THINK I HAVE T

WIGGLE FIDGETS

A STORY ABOUT ADHD AND OVERCOMING CHALLENGES

WORDS BY
BARBARA ESHAM

PICTURES BY
MIKE AND CARL GORDON

sourcebooks
eXplore

"David Sheldon, you are distracting your neighbor again," said Mrs. Gorski with her serious voice. "You are going to have to stop making that noise with your pencil!"

I tried to explain that I only wanted to see how many times I could roll my pencil to the very edge of my desk without it falling off, but Mrs. Gorski interrupted me.

"I do not need an explanation, David, but I do need you to pay attention in class."

Once again, everyone in the class was staring at me.

I get the feeling Mrs. Gorski gets frustrated with me. I can tell by the way her voice changes when she speaks to me. It's her "Speaking to David" voice.

I know that I can sometimes be a handful; I just don't know how to stop.

The problem is, I'm not thinking about paying attention when I'm not paying attention.

If I were thinking about paying attention when I'm not paying attention, I would definitely pay attention.

I want to pay attention but it is just so hard when an exciting idea pops into my head.

Nothing else seems important when there are ideas to think about.

Every day I do something that upsets Mrs. Gorski. I never mean to do it, but it happens anyway.

Like the time we had our first fire drill.

I really made her mad that day.

Mrs. Gorski told us to stand single file, on the line, in the parking lot. I really tried to pay attention and follow the instructions, but I got a really good idea...

I wanted to see how long I could

stand on one foot

with my eyes closed

with both hands on my shoulders

while hopping in place

while standing

single file on the line

in the parking lot.

I was following Mrs. Gorski's directions, except I was on one foot...until I fell down.

Maybe she was a little upset because our class was the only one that wasn't standing during the fire drill.

But that was nothing compared to
yesterday in the cafeteria.

It all started with a pudding cup and an idea.

I wasn't trying to make a mess. I just wanted
to see how much pressure the lid could take
before...well, you can imagine.

I didn't see Mrs. Gorski standing behind me, and I didn't think a pudding cup could make such a mess.

"What possesses you to do such things, David?" Mrs. Gorski asked with her extra frustrated "Speaking to David" voice.

I tried to explain I didn't think the pudding would shoot that far, but she interrupted me.

"David, I will be sending a note home to your parents."

I don't know why I do what I do!

I can always see the mistakes I make...
after I make them. But before they're
mistakes, they just seem like great ideas.

I wish I could stop myself.

I wish I would think a little more
before I test my great ideas.

That night I listened while my parents talked about Mrs. Gorski's letter.

"David just has the wiggle fidgets. I had the wiggle fidgets when I was a kid. I had so many ideas bouncing around in my mind that it was impossible for me to sit still," my dad told my mom.

"Mrs. Gorski wants to meet with us Monday afternoon," my mom replied.

I have until Monday to think of a plan,
and I know what I have to do.

I'll have to find a way to stop the wiggle fidgets!

I know I'm not the only kid struggling with the
wiggle fidgets.

THIS COULD BE MY GREATEST DISCOVERY YET!

I spent most of Saturday afternoon brainstorming.
I'm great at that. Brainstorming is one of my strengths.

I have to be careful that none of my solutions for the wiggle fidgets will be distracting to me or my class or Mrs. Gorski.

In other words, I have to think about consequences.

I hope my parents and Mrs. Gorski will be proud of me for a change.

Monday after school I went to my locker to get what I needed for the meeting: my notebook and my box of items to help with the wiggle fidgets.

I found my parents and Mrs. Gorski in the classroom.

Using my most serious voice, I said, "Mom, Dad, Mrs. Gorski, on Saturday I discovered exactly the problem might be. I learned some important information that has inspired me to come up with a solution for this very serious—but common—struggle."

I looked at my dad, and then I said,
"The problem I have is called the wiggle fidgets!
It is something that you can inherit from your
parents, or you can just have it.

"My dad had the wiggle fidgets
when he was a kid. The difference
is I have come up with a possible
cure. Or at least it's something
that might help a little. It took all
day on Saturday to develop it."

My parents and Mrs. Gorski just listened.

"I have come up with a few things that will help me pay attention better," I announced while spreading some note cards on the table. "These are my attention cards—patent pending."

"If I put one of these cards on my desk, it will remind me to focus and leave the distracting ideas and thoughts alone."

Focus and Listen

Attention!
SAVE THAT IDEA FOR LATER!

THINK about what we are WORKING ON!

What are the CONSEQUENCES?

"This way, Mrs. Gorski, you can save your voice and I can save myself from becoming embarrassed. Everyone in the class becomes distracted when you ask me to pay attention."

"But that's not my only idea for the wiggle fidgets. I also have a timer that counts down silently.

"I've discovered that, if I know exactly how long I need to pay attention, it keeps me from wondering about how long I need to pay attention."

I couldn't believe it; Mrs. Gorski was actually **SMILING AT ME!**

I have a feeling she likes my ideas.

Then, using my serious announcement voice, I said, "For the super wiggly fidget days, I need to have something to do. Even if it is just a small something to fidget with, like this stress ball.

"I've noticed that when I fidget with the stress ball at home, it actually helps me pay attention. I'm not sure exactly how it works, but I know it does."

I hoped Mrs. Gorski was still listening.

"Another way to help make the wiggle fidgets go away is to move just a little. Sometimes my legs feel like they are going to run away without me. If I could just hand out papers or, better yet, run your papers to the school office, my legs might not be so wiggly at my desk. I have also noticed that the more I get to move during recess, the less I move at my desk. Plus, recess seems to help my brain feel refreshed and ready to focus." I wanted to help Mrs. Gorski understand.

"Well, that's all I have for today. I will be available to answer questions if anyone has them," I said as I collected my items.

"David, I am quite impressed," Mrs. Gorski announced in a voice that wasn't frustrated. "I think your ideas are wonderful. We will start using them tomorrow. Of course we will have to keep your box of ideas from becoming a distraction for the rest of the class, but I am sure we can make this work."

"Your ideas might work well at home too," said my mom.

"David, you always come up with the most original ideas. You remind me of a kid that I used to know," my dad added with a smile.

"You know, Mrs. Gorski, I was thinking," I said, feeling quite confident.

"I think my ideas might help Jeremy too. He doesn't move around as much as I do, but I can tell that he gets tired of sitting sometimes, especially during social studies.

I also notice that Karina becomes distracted by Timmy when he acts silly.

Maybe some of the other kids in our class will wiggle and fidget less with a little help."

"I think your plan is going to help me manage the entire classroom's wiggle fidgets," Mrs. Gorski replied with a smile.

"I can remember when I had the wiggle fidgets. I couldn't wait to get up from my desk during science class to touch the project materials or look through the microscope.

"I can remember Mrs. Smith, my science teacher, telling me to sit still or I wouldn't get to do the science activity."

"Mrs. Gorski, you had the wiggle fidgets too?"

"David, many great minds come with the wiggle fidgets," she answered with a smile.

I noticed she wasn't using her frustrated "Speaking with David" voice anymore.

A NOTE TO CARING ADULTS
FROM DR. EDWARD HALLOWELL

New York Times national bestseller, former Harvard Medical School instructor, and current director of the Hallowell Center for Cognitive and Emotional Health

Fear is the great disabler. Fear is what keeps children from realizing their potential. It needs to be replaced with a feeling of I-know-I-can-make-progress-if-I-keep-trying-and-boy-do-I-ever-want-to-do-that!

One of the great goals of parents, teachers, and coaches should be to find areas in which a child might experience mastery, then make it possible for the child to feel this potent sensation. The feeling of mastery transforms a child from a reluctant, fearful learner into a self-motivated player. The mistake that parents, teachers, and coaches often make is that they demand mastery rather than lead children to it by helping them overcome the fear of failure. The best parents are great teachers. My definition of a great teacher is a person who can lead another person to mastery.

ARE YOU AN EVERYDAY GENIUS TOO?

Everyday geniuses are **creative,** STRONG, thoughtful, and sometimes learn a little differently from others. And that's what makes them so special!

In *I Think I Have the Wiggle Fidgets*, David struggles with paying attention. He often gets distracted and he usually doesn't know that he's done something wrong until after it happens. But David discovers there are ways that he can help himself to stay focused and that many great minds are the kinds that move and shake and don't stand still.

Have you ever struggled to pay attention or sit still? What happened?

In our story, David comes up with a plan to help him with his wiggle fidgets by using a few different techniques:

- Attention cards. If David puts a card on his desk, it will remind him to focus and leave his distracting thoughts alone.
- Silent timer. Using the silent timer helps David see exactly how long he needs to pay attention.
- Stress ball. For super wiggly fidget days, David needs something to do to help pay attention, like squishing a stress ball.

- Moving around. Sometimes just getting up and moving around the room can help David refocus his energy.

You can try using David's tricks but remember that there is no right or wrong method because every person is unique and learns differently. And not everything that works for David will work for you. Do you have a way that helps you focus your attention? Have you tried any ways that did not work so well? What happened?

If you or someone you know has ever struggled with focusing your attention, talk about it with a caring adult.

Remember, everyday geniuses are creative, strong, thoughtful, and sometimes learn a little differently from others. It's never a bad thing to be different—embracing and learning from our differences is what makes the world a better place!

ABOUT THE AUTHOR

Author Barbara Esham was one of those kids who couldn't resist performing a pressure test on a pudding cup. She has always been a "free association" thinker, finding life far more interesting while in a state of abstract thought. Barbara lives on the East Coast with her three daughters. Together, in Piagetian fashion, they have explored the ideas and theories behind the definitions of intelligence, creativity, learning, and success. Barb researches and writes from her home office in the spare time available between car pools, homework, and bedtime.

ABOUT THE ILLUSTRATORS

Cartooning has brought Mike Gordon acclaim in worldwide competitions, adding to his international reputation as a top humorous illustrator. Since 1993 he has continued his successful career based in California, gaining a nomination in the prestigious National Cartoonist Society Awards. Mike is the renowned illustrator for the wildly popular book series beginning with *Do Princesses Wear Hiking Boots?* Mike collaborates with his son Carl Gordon from across the world. They have been a team since 1999. Mike creates the line illustrations, and the color is applied by Carl using a graphics tablet and computer. Carl has a degree in graphic art and currently lives in Cape Town, South Africa, with his wife and kids.

Text © 2008, 2018, 2024 by Barbara Esham
Illustrations © 2008, 2018, 2024 by Mike Gordon
Illustrations by Mike and Carl Gordon
Cover design by Travis Hasenour
Cover and internal design © 2018, 2024 by Sourcebooks
Sourcebooks and the colophon are registered trademarks of Sourcebooks.

The story text was set in OpenDyslexic, a font specifically designed for readability with dyslexia.
The back matter was set in Adobe Garamond Pro.
Published by Sourcebooks eXplore, an imprint of Sourcebooks Kids
P.O. Box 4410, Naperville, Illinois 60567-4410
(630) 961-3900
sourcebookskids.com
Originally published as *Mrs. Gorski, I Think I Have the Wiggle Fidgets* in 2008 in the United States of America by Mainstream Connections Publishing. This edition issued based on the hardcover edition published in 2018 in the United States of America by Sourcebooks Kids.
Cataloging-in-Publication Data is on file with the Library of Congress.

Source of Production: Lightning Source, Inc., La Vergne, TN, USA
Date of Production: May 2024
Run Number: 5040831

Printed and bound in the United States of America.
LSI 10 9 8 7 6 5 4 3 2 1

9 781728 289410